Barbie™

MYSTERY FILES #8

Mystery
Unplugged

Want to read more of Barbie's Mystery Files? Don't miss the first two books in the series, The Haunted Mansion Mystery and The Mystery of the Jeweled Mask.

Barbie™

MYSTERY FILES #3

Mystery Unplugged

By Linda Aber

SCHOLASTIC INC.

New York   Toronto   London   Auckland   Sydney
Mexico City   New Delhi   Hong Kong   Buenos Aires

ISBN 0-439-37206-2

Designed by Peter Koblish
Photography by Tom Wolfson, Shirley Oshirogata, Jake Johnson,
Jeremy Lloyd, Steve Toth, Judy Tsuno, and Lisa Collins

12 11 10 9 8 7 6 5 4 3 2 1   2 3 4 5 6/0

Printed in the U.S.A.   40
First Scholastic printing, April 2002

You can help Barbie solve this mystery! Flip to page 64 and use the reporter's notebook to jot down facts, clues, and suspects in the case. Add more notes as you and Barbie uncover clues. If you can figure out who the culprit is, you'll be on your way to becoming a star reporter, just like Barbie!

Barbie™

MYSTERY FILES #3

Mystery Unplugged

Chapter 1

· ·

ASSIGNMENT TO ROCK

"Yeah, I am the one, the one and only one, yeah, I am the only, only, only, only one. Yeah, yeah, oh, yeah . . ."

"Oh, no!" Barbie and Christie groaned together. The screeching, whining, off-key song blaring from the car radio hurt their ears more with each note.

"It's that song again!" Christie exclaimed. "Everywhere we go, they're playing the same 'yeah, yeah, oh, yeah' song."

Barbie laughed as her friend covered her ears to block out the last sour notes of the song. "I'd cover my ears, too," she said, "if I didn't have to keep both hands on the steering wheel."

Christie smiled. She and Barbie had been friends since they were very young. Together with two other friends, Kira and Becky, they'd participated

1

in the same clubs and gone to the same sleep-overs. All of them felt very lucky to have grown up in Willow, and they all came back to Willow after college.

"*Yeah, I am the one, the one and only one, yeah, I am the only, only, only one.*"

"The DJs must all be asleep at their jobs! How can they keep playing a song that's so bad?" Christie said.

"There's no way a DJ could sleep through this!" Barbie added.

"*Yeah, I am the one, the one and only one, yeah, I am the only, only, only one. Oh, yeah!*"

"Oh, yeah! Over at last!" Christie exclaimed, taking her hands away from her ears.

As the song ended, Barbie steered her shiny red convertible toward the parking lot of the Willow Music World store. While she parked the car next to a black motorcycle with a license plate that read SPIN PRO, the radio announcer went into the usual fast-talking disc jockey chatter.

"You're listening to WSQR radio, and that was 'Oh, Yeah,' a new song by the Jammers! The Jam-

2

mers is just one of the many bands that will be featured on the hit TV show *The Battle of the Bands*," the announcer continued. "Tickets for the filming of the show are going fast. Don't miss out on your chance to be part of the live studio audience when *The Battle of the Bands* is filmed next week on the campus of All State University!"

"Ha!" Christie said. "The Jammers are going to be one of the contestants on *The Battle of the Bands*! Do you think they have any chance of winning?"

"Who knows?" Barbie replied. "The amazing thing is that a band that's so bad can get so much attention! It sure makes me wonder what they've got going for them in person. I guess I'll just have to wait and see what happens when we go to the filming of the show."

"Really?" Christie exclaimed. "Are you going to see the filming?"

"It's my next reporting assignment for the *Willow Gazette*," Barbie explained. "I'm covering the filming of *The Battle of the Bands*. My editor wants me to try to find an interesting, behind-the-scenes story and interview the winning band. The band

3

that wins the final contest on *The Battle of the Bands* will sign a recording contract with Kingston Studios. I hope to be the first to break the story in print. This is one assignment I don't want to miss."

"I don't blame you," Christie said. "I sure wish my job would send me on such a great assignment. I'd love to see all the bands in the contest. I can't wait to find out who wins the final battle."

"Well," Barbie replied, "I guess we'll both find out together."

"*We* will?" Christie asked. "Together?"

Barbie grinned. "Oh, did I forget to tell you that I have a surprise for you? We're going to All State University to meet the bands and see the filming of *The Battle of the Bands*!"

"Oh, Barbie," Christie said. "I'd love to go, but I have to talk to the photography studio and see if I can take time off from my job."

"This *is* your job, Christie," Barbie explained. "My editor at the newspaper wanted me to bring a photographer along. I already talked to your booking agent at the photography studio. You're going to be my freelance photographer on the assignment!"

"Wow!" Christie said excitedly. "I can't believe I'm really going to see *The Battle of the Bands* live! This is amazing!"

"I thought you'd like it." Barbie smiled. "It'll be so much fun to work together. And meanwhile," Barbie continued, getting out of the car, "every good reporter knows you can't do a story without doing some research first. I'm hoping Corey will have a list of all the bands that will be competing in *The Battle of the Bands*. My assignment really begins right here at Willow Music World."

Chapter 2

• • • • • • • • • • • • • • • • • • • •

PREVIEW TO THE BATTLE

The two friends walked up the gravel path to the front door of the music store. A stocky man rushed by them. He wore goggles and a black motorcycle jacket and was pulling a black helmet over his head as he ran. Without looking back, he jumped on the motorcycle, kick-started it, and sped out of the parking lot toward the main highway.

"Whoa!" Barbie gasped. "There's a man on a mission! He sure is in a hurry!" She pulled the store door open — then groaned when the familiar strains of "Oh, Yeah" drifted out. "Can you believe it?" Barbie said, laughing. "This song is everywhere!"

"Hey, Barbie, hey, Christie," said a young man behind the counter. He pushed a lock of long, sun-

6

streaked blond hair out of his eyes and smiled. "Looking for something special today?"

"Hi, Corey," Barbie and Christie greeted the store's owner together.

"As a matter of fact, we *are* looking for something special," Barbie said.

"Well, what can I do for you?" Corey asked.

Barbie spoke up. "My newspaper is sending Christie and me to cover *The Battle of the Bands* at the university," she said. "I'm looking for a list of the bands that will be in the competition. Do you have any advance information?"

"Sure do," Corey said. "That's the great thing about owning a music store. I get all the advance information, and I even get advance copies of new CDs. In fact, that guy left me one, and I got another one in the morning mail. It was from a group called 4 to Go. Sad to say, the CD arrived broken! I heard part of the song on the radio once, though, and I liked it. They should have hand-delivered it like this group did."

"Is it a group that's going to be in the battle?" Barbie asked.

Corey read the label on the CD and laughed. "Well, how about that! It's the Jammers!"

"That's who's on the radio right now!" Christie exclaimed. "But they sure won't win the battle."

"Who knows?" Corey said. "Stranger things have happened. Nobody knows who will win until the bands actually compete against one another. And once a band wins on *The Battle of the Bands,* they're guaranteed to make it big. But I can tell you one thing," he continued. "I don't think it'll be the Jammers, either!" Corey held up the Jammers' CD. It had a fancy gold label on it.

"May I see that?" Barbie asked.

"Sure," Corey said, handing the disc to her. "The packaging is pretty good for an amateur group, but it will take a lot more than packaging to make these guys successful."

Barbie examined the CD. Then she took out her reporter's notebook and copied down the information from the label. It read, *The Jammers, distributed by Spin Productions.*

"Wow. You're right about the packaging," Barbie remarked. "Everything goes together, right down to the license plate on that guy's motorcycle. It was SPIN PRO, and the CD is distributed by Spin Productions."

Christie laughed. "Hey!" she said. "The reporting assignment doesn't start until tomorrow!"

Barbie shook her head. "Not for me," she replied. "The minute I get the assignment is the minute I begin working! It's just a little difficult to write with my hands over my ears."

Corey and Christie laughed. Barbie blocked her ears as the speakers screeched out the last notes of "Oh, Yeah."

"Change the station, please!" Barbie moaned.

"It's no use," Corey said. "This is WTXR, but all the radio stations are playing that song. That guy really is promoting his group!"

"Was he one of the band members?" Barbie asked.

"Why else would he hand-deliver the CD to radio stations, music stores, and anyone else who might play it? All the stations are previewing songs from the different bands in the contest. That's how I heard 4 to Go. Now there's a really good group. Their song, 'Forever and a Day,' is coming up next. Have you heard it?"

"Not yet," Barbie said.

As soon as "Oh, Yeah" ended, a commercial for *The Battle of the Bands* rattled off a bunch of band names. The last band mentioned was 4 to Go. "Now, as promised," the disc jockey said, "I'm going to play a sure hit in the making, 'Forever and a Day,' by 4 to Go. Keep your radio dial set to WTXR, where the hits keep coming at ya!"

The music began with a guitar riff over a keyboard, bass guitar, and easy drumbeat. Four voices started singing in perfect harmony. Barbie, Christie, and Corey listened attentively. *"You are my dream. You are my special one. Promise you'll stay forever and a day."*

"Oh, it's beautiful!" Barbie whispered.

"I saw your face. And I knew right away. Our love would last forever and a day. Now that you're here and I am —" Suddenly, the song was cut off.

"What happened?" Christie asked, startled by the abrupt interruption.

The DJ's voice blasted from the speakers. "Sorry about that, listeners," he said. "The phone lines are lighting up. I know you're all calling to find out what happened to the rest of that song. Our copy seems to be damaged. Oops, my engineer is holding up a sign telling me the CD has been badly scratched. We'll try to get another copy and play it again for you later. Time now for an update on the traffic report."

Corey flipped the radio off. "Oh, well," he said. "At least you heard some of it."

"Yes," Barbie said. "I think 4 to Go is going to give the Jammers some stiff competition when *The Battle of the Bands* begins."

"Oh, that reminds me," Corey said. "You came in asking for a list of the bands in the competition. Here's what I've got." He handed Barbie a schedule sheet listing all the bands and the different times they would be playing.

Barbie ran her finger down the list and found 4 to Go. The schedule said they'd be the first band to play on day one of the two-day event. "Looks like we'll have to get there early tomorrow, Christie," Barbie said. "At least we're sure to hear the whole song if we're seeing them in person!"

"Let me know how it goes," Corey said. "I'll be looking forward to reading your review."

"Good deal," Barbie said. "Thanks for the list and the heads-up on 4 to Go."

The two friends said good-bye to Corey and returned to the car. As soon as Barbie turned the key in the ignition, she switched the radio to another station. "I'm just curious to see what the other stations are playing," she explained. To her surprise, she heard four voices singing, *"You are my dream. You are my special one. Promise you'll stay forever and a day. I saw your face. And I knew right away. Our love would last forever and a day. Now that you're here and I am —"*

The song was suddenly cut off in exactly the same spot as before! "I'm sorry about that," the DJ apologized. "I guess we've just got a bad copy of that song. I'd say 4 to Go isn't going to make it big if that's the kind of demo CD they're sending out!"

"Isn't that a strange coincidence that two CDs would be damaged at the same exact spot?" Christie asked.

Barbie cocked her head and stared at the radio. She was already deep in thought. "Maybe it's a coincidence," she finally said. "Or maybe this Battle of the Bands is beginning early!"

12

Chapter 3

• • • • • • • • • • • • • • • • • • •

CHECKING IN

As they had planned, Barbie and Christie arrived in the town of Manchester early the next morning. A banner that read MANCHESTER ROCKS! WELCOME TO *THE BATTLE OF THE BANDS!* hung across the main street of the town.

"Well." Barbie laughed as she drove under the sign and up the hill to their hotel. "I guess they've handed the whole town over to the musicians!"

"And to the television crews," Christie added, pointing to a huge trailer topped with satellite dishes. It was parked next to the university's performing arts center. *THE BATTLE OF THE BANDS* MOBILE UNIT was stenciled in black-and-red letters on the side of the long equipment truck.

The Manchester Inn was just up the road from

the performing arts center. Barbie pulled into the hotel parking lot, stopped the car in the middle of the lot, and looked around at the strangest group of cars, vans, and buses she'd ever seen in one place.

A purple compact car with the name TUNED OUT painted on the sides was parked next to a plain tan-colored car. Wedged between the tan car and a NO PARKING sign was a beat-up old sedan with the words 4 TO GO, obviously painted by an amateur, on the driver's door. There was a sleek black limousine with the license plate BATTLE parked next to a purple minibus with THE JAMMERS airbrushed on both sides.

"Here's your first photograph, Christie," Barbie said. "Would you mind getting a picture of all the different bands' cars? I think we're staying at the same place as a lot of the bands and the television crew."

Christie took a few photographs, then followed Barbie to the front desk to check in. A young man standing behind the desk smiled as they approached. The name tag on his blue uniform blazer read CHARLES.

"Good morning, ladies. Are you checking in?" he asked.

"Yes," Barbie replied. "We have a reservation under the name Roberts. Barbie Roberts."

"Oh, yes, Ms. Roberts," the young man said. "You're with the *Gazette*, aren't you? I'm sure you're in town to cover the big battle, right?"

"Yes to both your questions," Barbie said, smiling. "From the looks of your parking lot, it would appear that we're not the only ones here for the battle."

"You can say that again," Charles said with a laugh. "Everyone who has ever even *thought* of performing in a band or singing solo is here trying to meet the right people. I'm sure you know that it's really difficult to break into the music business. It's all who you know."

"Well, I hope talent is important, too," Christie added.

Charles smiled. "Talent and contacts," he said. "But I'm not worried about either. I don't sing and I don't play an instrument. You won't see me trying to push my way into the music business. You'll

15

just see me here, telling you that you'll be in Room 10. That's down the hall and to the left." He handed Barbie two room keys. "Enjoy your stay with us!"

"Thank you," Barbie said, taking the keys. "I'm sure we will."

Barbie and Christie went directly to their room, dropped off their bags, and headed right back out. Charles was on the telephone, but he waved as they passed by the desk. "With all those musicians trying to make it to the top," he said, "it could be dangerous out there! Be careful."

"Thanks, Charles," Barbie said. "We'll do our best not to get caught in the crossfire of all the battling bands!"

No sooner had the words left Barbie's mouth than she was almost trampled by a curly-haired teenage boy in a gray sweatshirt running into the lobby. "Are they here yet?" the boy said breathlessly to Charles. "Is anyone good here yet?"

The smile on Charles's face disappeared. "I told you before not to come back here," he said to the excited teen. "Even if some of the bands are here, we can't have our guests being bothered by

16

people off the street! Now, please, I'm asking you for the last time, go outside and find something else to do!"

The boy looked disappointed, but not defeated. He ran past the girls again and out the door. "Something tells me he'll catch up with one of the bands somehow," Barbie laughed.

"Well, it won't be inside the Manchester Inn," Charles declared. "See you later, ladies."

They stepped outside and, to their surprise, they heard a familiar-sounding song coming from somewhere down the street. *"Yeah, I am the one, the one and only one, yeah, I am the only, only, only, only one. Yeah, yeah, oh, yeah . . ."*

"Uh-oh," Barbie groaned, covering her ears. "There's the *real* danger!"

Chapter 4

• • • • • • • • • • • • • • • • • • • •

LOST IN THE CROWD

"Okay," Christie said, laughing at her friend. "You can uncover your ears now. The music is gone."

"Whew!" Barbie replied. "Now, back to business." She had her reporter's notebook and a tape recorder in her leather shoulder bag. Stopping for a moment, Barbie reached into her bag and pulled out two press passes. She clipped one onto her jacket and handed the other to Christie. "Clip this onto your camera bag," she said. "These passes will identify us as members of the media. Guard it as if it were made of gold, and make sure you display it at all times. I'm certain security will be pretty tight with all the television and music equipment on campus. As long as we're wearing our press passes, we'll be allowed behind the scenes and backstage."

Barbie and Christie walked down University Boulevard toward the center of town. The main attraction of the small town was All State University. The road was lined with dormitories and academic buildings, as well as local houses, businesses, and residents.

Stores and restaurants aimed at college students' interests lined the main street. The sidewalks bustled with groups of college kids talking and laughing as they headed for their classes or stopped for breakfast at one of the snack bars or cafés along the way.

It looked like many other college towns, except for all the musicians in town for *The Battle of the Bands*. Barbie and Christie walked through groups of young people carrying guitar cases, keyboard cases, cymbals, microphone stands, heavy guitar amplifiers, and many other kinds of instruments, large and small.

On one corner, a girl with long dark hair played guitar and sang an upbeat love song. She had glitter on her face and a pink feather boa thrown around her neck, making her look glamorous. Passersby tossed coins into her open guitar case and wished her luck with her music career. Barbie and Christie stopped and listened for a minute.

Christie took a photo of the girl, who smiled and kept playing. Barbie placed a generous number of coins in the guitar case.

"Thanks," said the girl, still strumming her guitar.

"Good luck," Barbie said. "Hope to see you again." She and Christie continued moving through the crowds.

They walked around town for more than an hour. As they walked, they saw the same poster tacked up everywhere. It was a photo of a phone booth with six guys crammed inside. The lettering across the top of the phone booth said THE JAMMERS.

"This is amazing!" Barbie said, pointing to the fifth poster they saw. "If I didn't know better, I'd think the only band competing in the contest was going to be the Jammers! Are they the only band who knows how to put out publicity?"

As if on cue, the purple minibus belonging to the Jammers rounded the corner onto the main street at just that moment. A loudspeaker system on its roof screeched out "Oh, Yeah."

Barbie and Christie recognized the band mem-

20

bers inside the bus from the posters they'd seen. Instead of being crammed inside a phone booth, they were crowded into the minibus! They looked just as scruffy in person as they did on the posters. The only difference was that none of them was smiling.

"Wow," Christie said to Barbie. "They don't look too friendly."

"No," Barbie agreed, "they don't. But these guys sure do!" She had stopped in front of a message board on the side of the campus bookstore. "Finally, a poster for another band," she said. "And look! It's 4 to Go!"

Barbie and Christie stepped forward to get a closer look at the photograph. The four clean-shaven, well-groomed band members in the picture smiled as they posed in 4 to Go T-shirts. Their names and instruments were listed under their pictures: lead guitar and lead singer Jake Colton, bass guitar and backup Ace Frye, drummer Kevin Taylor, and keyboard player Dave Williams.

"Well, it's sure good to know that another band is in the contest!" Barbie joked. "And, hey, they look as good as their music sounds!"

Christie held up her press pass and giggled. "Interview time!" she said, fluttering her eyelashes. "I think we definitely need to meet this group! I might already be a fan!"

Barbie laughed at her friend's sudden interest in the group of four handsome young men. "Take a picture. It lasts longer," she said.

"Great idea!" Christie said, taking out her camera. "I think I will!" She focused on the poster and snapped a close-up of it. As she stepped back to get another shot, someone bumped her roughly from behind. Startled, Christie swung around, snapping a picture of nothing by mistake. She almost dropped the camera, but she didn't see who'd run into her.

Christie was flustered. She checked her camera equipment for damage before checking herself. The camera was fine, and so was she. "I'm okay," she said. "It's crowded. It was just an accident."

"Maybe," Barbie replied. "But whoever did *that*, did it on purpose!" She pointed to Christie's camera bag.

"Oh, no!" Christie exclaimed.

"Oh, yes," Barbie said with a worried look on her face. "I'm afraid your press pass has been stolen!"

Chapter 5

●●●●●●●●●●●●●●●●●●●●

MIKE PARKER

"Stolen?" Christie cried in disbelief. She was already searching the ground for the missing press pass. "It must be around here somewhere. It probably just got knocked off when I was bumped."

Barbie shook her head. "I don't think it was an accident," she said. "A press pass could be very useful to anyone who wants to get backstage or inside without a ticket."

"Oh, Barbie," Christie said woefully. "What should we do?"

"Don't worry," Barbie said, patting her friend's arm. "The first thing we need to do is let the security people and the manager of the television crew know that your pass was stolen. Maybe they can issue you a temporary pass."

Barbie checked the performance schedule Corey

23

had given her the day before. "4 to Go is scheduled to appear in forty-five minutes," she said. "We'd better hurry over to the performing arts center so we can take care of this right away."

Barbie led the way up the hill to the performing arts center. She and Christie retraced their steps, looking for the pass along the way. The girl who had been singing on the corner was gone. In her place was a young guy playing a jaunty tune on an Irish tin whistle. He seemed to be playing more for his own amusement than for the people passing by. Barbie and Christie hurried past him toward the performing arts center.

As with any big event, fans of all ages were already lining up for tickets and promotional items such as the bumper stickers, T-shirts, and buttons that were being handed out or sold. Even though her mind was full of questions about who might have taken the press pass and why, Barbie made mental notes of the scene around her. The crowd was interesting because it was made up of so many different types of people. Some were dressed in khaki pants or jeans and plaid shirts. Others wore all black and had dyed their hair green or pink or orange. There were girls with short, spiked hair and boys with hair down to their shoulders. It was a lively mix of country, rock, rap, folk, and punk music fans. The scene reminded Barbie more of a carnival than a music concert.

There was even more excitement over by *The Battle of the Bands* equipment trailer. "Look!" Barbie said, pointing to the crowd flocking around a handsome, dark-haired man wearing a leather jacket and black pants. He looked about five years older than Barbie and Christie. "It's Mike Parker," Barbie said to Christie. "He's the host of *The Battle of the Bands*. He used to be the lead singer in his own band. I must own every album he ever made!"

"Oh, yes!" Christie replied, trying to see over the heads of the group of fans around him. "But I don't suppose I can get any closer than the fans without my press pass."

Barbie linked arms with her friend. "Stick with me," she said, cheerfully pulling Christie closer to the gathering.

Excited fans held up paper and pens, shouting, "Hey, Mike! Over here, Mike! May I have your autograph, pleeeeeease?"

25

"Gee," Christie said, peering over the heads of the crowd. "He's even better looking in person than he is on TV!"

Mike Parker signed his autograph for the crowd around him. Suddenly, the curly-haired boy from the inn lobby pushed his way to the front of the crowd and begged for an autograph. "Please!" he pleaded, shoving a scrap of paper and a pen under Mike Parker's nose.

"Wow," Christie said. "That kid doesn't give up! He's a real groupie. He'll do anything to be near a celebrity."

Barbie and Christie watched as the show host politely signed his autograph. He handed the paper back to the guy, then decided to end the autograph session before the crowd got out of control. His smile was genuine as he thanked everyone for coming to cheer for all the bands competing in *The Battle of the Bands.*

The curly-haired autograph-seeker ran from the group of fans shouting, "I got it! I got Mike Parker's autograph!"

Mike Parker shook his head with a smile and turned to go inside the performing arts center.

Barbie realized he was going to walk right past her and Christie, and she couldn't resist the opportunity to ask for an interview.

"Hello, Mr. Parker," she called to him. "I'm Barbie Roberts, a reporter for the *Willow Gazette*, and this is my photographer and friend, Christie. Would it be possible for us to take a photograph and do an interview?"

"Please," the man said, smiling again, "call me Mike. I'd be glad to talk with you and have a picture taken, too! I don't see *your* press pass, though, young lady," he kidded Christie.

"I'm afraid someone may have stolen it just a little while ago," Christie explained.

"Yes, in fact, we were just about to try to find someone in charge who could issue a temporary pass," Barbie added.

Mike offered an arm to each of them. "Perhaps you'd allow me to be your temporary pass for the moment," he said. "It's time to introduce you to Clyde, the production manager. He's in charge of everything, onstage and off. The motto around here is, 'To get inside, talk to Clyde!' And that's just what we'll do."

27

Chapter 6

• • • • • • • • • • • • • • • • • • •

BEHIND THE SCENES

The girls gratefully accepted Mike's offer to escort them inside the performing arts center. It was cool to bypass the long line at the front of the building as he led them around to a stage door on the side.

"There's Clyde Andrews," Mike said, pointing to a ponytailed man wearing a red satin jacket with *The Battle of the Bands* embroidered across the back. He was at the door, turning some people away and letting others inside.

"The press pass is a pretty important piece of jewelry to wear around here," Mike said. "It's the next best thing to having a job on the show. We can't be too careful when there are so many stars around. Some of those fans can get a little crazy. Clyde decides who gets in and who doesn't. His word is final. Great guy, Clyde is. Worked his way up from being a roadie — a setup guy. He started with a small job, and now he's in charge of everything."

"Hey, Mike!" the ponytailed man said as the three approached him.

"Clyde!" Mike greeted him. "I've brought a reporter and photographer with me. Barbie and Christie, meet Clyde. He's our famous door guard and production manager."

"It's all behind-the-scenes stuff," Clyde said modestly. "This guy's the real star. He's done it all — had a band, been a lead singer, hosted the show." While he talked, Clyde looked at Barbie's pass. "So you're from the *Gazette,* eh?" he said. "One of the best local papers in the country. Any publicity you can give the show will be welcome. I'll be glad to get you an interview with some of the bands in the competition. Just let me know which ones you'd like to speak with."

"Thank you, Clyde," Barbie said. "I can tell you right now I'm interested in talking with a group called 4 to Go. Do you know them?"

"Yeah," Clyde replied a little less warmly. "They're

all right, although they're always having trouble of one kind or another. They're first up today. If they show up, that is." He changed the subject by turning his attention to Christie. "No press pass for you?"

Mike spoke up for Christie. "She's with the *Gazette,* too, Clyde," he said. "She's the photographer. You'll have to trust me on this one. Her pass was stolen. Have you got a temporary one she can wear?"

"No need, now that you've introduced us," Clyde replied. "Any friend of Mike's is a friend of mine."

"Thanks, Clyde," Mike said, turning to Barbie and Christie. "Ladies, after you."

Mike led the way past Clyde and into the backstage section of the arts center. The place was bustling with electrical workers, sound and lighting technicians, makeup artists, segment producers, and musicians. Each of them had a greeting for the host of the show.

Barbie and Christie felt very privileged to be escorted by Mike and were even more pleased when he began introducing them to the different band members. "Ladies," he said as they approached a group made up of three guys and two girls, "I'd like you to meet the members of Tuned Out — Allie, Melody, Tom, Sammy, and Dave. Tuned Out, meet the reporter and photographer from the *Willow Gazette*."

"I hope you enjoy our performance," said Allie.

"What do you think of our name?" asked Tom.

"Very clever," Barbie replied. "And I'll bet I won't want to tune you out!"

Christie took photographs of the group and Barbie jotted down notes about how they got started, where they were from, how long they'd been together, and where they hoped to be in their careers a year from then.

Mike looked at his watch and said it was time to let the band get ready for the show. "Good luck in the battle!" Barbie called to Tuned Out as she and Christie followed Mike across the staging area.

"I've got to leave you for now," Mike said. "I'll come back just before show time and put you in two of the best seats in the house. We've closed off the front row for VIPs. But for now, feel free to wander around in this area. There's the Jammers over in the corner," he said, pointing to the scruffy guys they'd seen on the main street. "Go ahead and introduce yourselves and I'll see you later."

Barbie only saw five Jammers, but the sixth and scruffiest one came out from behind a curtain and joined the others. He whispered something to the others and then they all strutted over to another group Barbie and Christie both recognized — 4 to Go.

To their surprise, the members of the Jammers purposely bumped into the members of 4 to Go. "Sorry," the scruffiest Jammer said, a bit too loudly. "I guess you got in my way." He kept walking with the rest of the group following close behind.

"Did you see that?" Christie said. "They did that on purpose!"

"Yes," Barbie said. "I did see it. Let's go introduce ourselves. I'd rather talk to them than to the Jammers." Barbie led the way and walked right up to the band.

The four musicians looked exactly the same in

person as they did on the poster. Jake, the lead singer, was tall and blond; Ace, the bassist, was the same height as Jake but with jet-black hair; Kevin, the drummer, was medium height with red hair; and Dave, the keyboard player, was short with brown hair. Each had his own individual look, but all four of them flashed bright smiles at Barbie as soon as she introduced herself and Christie.

"We're really looking forward to hearing your performance," Barbie said, deciding not to mention the incident she'd witnessed.

"You've heard of us?" Jake asked in amazement.

"Did you see our poster?" Ace asked.

"Or hear our song on the radio?" Kevin said hopefully.

"Actually, we've done all three — heard of you, seen your poster, and heard at least a line or two of your song on the radio," Barbie said. "But unfortunately, the radio station we were listening to had a damaged copy of your CD, so we only heard a little bit of the song."

A look of dismay crossed Jake's face, and he shook his head. "We've been hearing that from other people, too," he said. "Something must have happened between the time we made the CDs and the time the radio stations received them."

"I'm sure you'll make up for it with your performance," Christie said, trying to cheer them all up. "Mind if I take some pictures?"

All four members of the band smiled. They posed willingly and answered Barbie's interview questions openly and honestly. They'd met in college and formed a band. They played at local clubs to earn money to pay their own way through school. It hadn't been easy, but they hoped the hard work and long hours were finally going to pay off.

"If we win on *The Battle of the Bands*, that is," Ace said.

"We're keeping our fingers crossed," Jake added. "I'm afraid if we don't make it here, we'll have to give up the band. The money has run out."

"This is our big chance," Kevin said. "It's all or nothing."

Barbie smiled at them and wished them luck again. "We'll be cheering for you," she said.

"Thanks," said all four guys at once.

34

"And if things go well," Jake added, "maybe you two would help us celebrate with a dinner on us?"

"That would be great," Christie said. "I can show you the photos then, too."

"Okay, girls and boys," Mike said, coming up behind them. "It's show time! Band, take your places onstage, and ladies, follow me!"

Chapter 7

• • • • • • • • • • • • • • • • • • •

THE MYSTERY FAN

Mike showed Barbie and Christie to front-row seats reserved for record company scouts and VIPs. Excited laughter and chatter carried through the huge auditorium. "Enjoy the show," Mike told them. Then he disappeared backstage again.

A few minutes later, the theater lights grew dim. A director spoke through a headset microphone to the crew in charge of filming. "Okay, music intro on three, and roll film! One . . . two . . . three!"

A flashing APPLAUSE sign lit up above the stage. The girls clapped with the rest of the audience. Then Mike ran onstage, smiling, and spoke directly into the television cameras. "Hello, music fans! Welcome to the final phase of *The Battle of the Bands*! We've already auditioned more than thirty bands for the program. Now we're down to the fi-

36

nal five contestants as they compete for the grand prize — a recording contract from Kingston Studios. This battle today will pick the two top bands and the runners-up. Here to kick off today's battle is a band that some say is favored to win. It's made up of four talented young guys — Jake Colton, Ace Frye, Kevin Taylor, and Dave Williams! Let's hear it for 4 to Go!"

"Finally, we'll get to hear the whole song!" Barbie whispered excitedly.

The audience applauded again as the curtain went up. Mike stepped to the side of the stage and gestured toward the four musicians as they began singing "Forever and a Day."

"You are my dream. You are my special one. Promise you'll stay forever and a day," Ace sang.

"Oh, they sound fabulous!" Christie exclaimed softly. "They're sure to win. They sound like they've been playing together for years!"

"I saw your face. And I knew right away. Our love would last forever and a day. Now that you're here and I am —"

Suddenly, the spotlights flickered. Screeching feedback from the microphones sent an ear-piercing, high-pitched sound through the whole auditorium. A loud popping sound came from one of the amplifiers onstage, and sparks flew from the cord connecting the amplifier to the lead guitar.

The audience screamed. Mike Parker tried to calm them through a microphone that was no longer working. There was a last big *BAM* that deafened the audience and the whole sound system blew out. 4 to Go's performance was a total disaster!

"Wow!" Christie gasped as the houselights flicked back on. "Everything seemed to blow out at once! Do you think the guys in the band are all right?"

As if to answer her question, Mike Parker came back onstage, this time with a microphone that worked. "Ladies and gentlemen," he said, "due to technical difficulties with 4 to Go, another band will be taking over in the opening spot. 4 to Go is out of the running, but let's hear it for the Jammers!"

The lights went down again and the Jammers were standing in place of 4 to Go. They immediately began playing *"Yeah, I am the one, the one and only one, yeah, I am the only, only, only, only one. Yeah, yeah, oh, yeah . . ."*

"Gee," Barbie said over the first line of the song, "If 4 to Go didn't have bad luck, they wouldn't have any luck at all!"

"I guess that's what Clyde meant," Christie said. "Nothing seems to be going well for them — first the scratched CDs, now technical problems. What could have caused all that to happen?"

"I don't know," Barbie said. "But I know who will. I'm going to call Kira on my cell phone. With all her experience at the Willow Town Theater, she should have some idea about how that could happen. I'll be right back."

"You're leaving me here with the Jammers!" Christie said in mock horror.

"Oh, yeah, yeah, yeah," Barbie joked as she slipped out of her seat and headed back toward the lobby.

As the Jammers continued their performance, the audience quieted down and listened as politely as they could. Murmurs of disapproval could be heard all through the theater.

Barbie was only gone for a couple of minutes. She returned to her seat in plenty of time to hear more of the Jammers.

"What did Kira say?" Christie whispered.

"In a nutshell," Barbie whispered back, "she said there was no way so many different things going wrong at once could be an accident. In other words," Barbie continued, "someone must have rigged things ahead of time so that everything would blow out at once!"

"Oh, Barbie!" Christie exclaimed. "That's terrible!"

"And speaking of terrible," Barbie said, looking up at the stage where the Jammers were screaming out their song, "on a terrible scale from one to ten, this group is about a 9.5!"

There was only one person in the audience who seemed to be enjoying the Jammers' performance. He had just slipped into a seat across the aisle from Barbie and Christie in the non-VIP section. "Yeah, yeah, yeah!" he sang along with the Jammers.

Barbie nudged Christie gently and pointed at the screamer. Christie's eyes opened wide. The Jammers fan in the front row wore the same gray hooded sweatshirt as the curly-haired groupie they'd seen begging for Mike Parker's autograph. His hood was up now, hiding his curly hair. He bobbed up and down in his seat, clapping his hands to the beat of the "Oh, Yeah" song.

"How did he get a front-row seat, I wonder?" Christie asked.

As the fan jumped up and down in his seat, something shiny flipped over his shoulder. It was Christie's press pass, clipped to the strings of his gray hooded sweatshirt!

Chapter 8

• • • • • • • • • • • • • • • • • • • •

THE DISCOVERY

Barbie eyed the press pass as it bounced up and down while the excited fan danced. "Christie," she whispered, "the song is ending. You wait here. I'm going to move across the aisle and sit behind him. He's not going to get away with this!"

"Okay," Christie said.

Barbie was already making her way through the darkened auditorium. She slid out of her seat and crept across the aisle. It was so dark, the boy didn't notice as she took the seat behind him and leaned over his left shoulder. "Excuse me," she said as he applauded wildly at the end of the Jammers' performance. "Excuse me," she said again, louder this time.

The boy didn't turn around, but he froze in his seat.

42

"I think you have something that doesn't belong to you," Barbie said through the hood covering his ear. "That press pass belongs to my friend!"

Before Barbie could get another word out, the boy bolted from his seat. He headed for the side aisle. Barbie moved quickly, but the boy was too fast. He had already disappeared.

Onstage, Mike announced the next group. There was no time to stop and watch them, though. Barbie guessed the boy had slipped behind the curtain, and she followed him.

The curtain actually covered a tiny vestibule area and a heavy steel door. Carefully, Barbie pushed open the door and went inside.

The steel door closed slowly behind her, sealing Barbie in a long, dimly lit, and deadly silent hallway. It was clear from the padded walls and doors labeled STUDIO that this was the area of the performing arts center where musicians could practice without being heard. The padding soundproofed the hall, keeping any noise from reaching the stage or auditorium. *In fact,* Barbie thought, *musicians could scream at the top of their lungs and never be heard in a soundproof area like this.*

That realization made her look over her shoulder nervously. She half-expected the curly-haired boy to jump out at her. But he didn't.

Barbie looked down the long hallway. A red light over an emergency exit door at the very end of the hallway cast an eerie glow. There were doors on both sides of the hallway. *He could be in any one of these rooms*, Barbie thought.

Barbie started with the first door on the left. She swung it open slowly, and a cat meowed as it ran past her. The door led to a storage room filled with chairs stacked one on top of another and music stands lined up along the wall. Barbie flipped on the light switch. The boy wasn't there.

Barbie stood still and listened for a moment. Hearing nothing, she went down the hallway and peeked into each room she came to. They were all soundproof practice rooms, and all were empty except for unused musical equipment. The room at the end of the hall next to the emergency exit was locked. "Well, I guess he didn't come in here after all," Barbie said to herself.

She headed back to the steel door at the other end of the long hallway. But then, to her surprise, the emergency exit door opened! *He's coming back in!* Barbie thought.

Barbie slipped inside one of the practice rooms, leaving the door slightly ajar so she could peek out. This thief was up to something and Barbie was determined to catch him in the act.

The shadowy figure stood in front of the locked door. The dim lighting made it impossible to see his movements clearly, but Barbie heard the muffled sound of a key rattling against a lock. The door opened and the stealthy figure went inside the room. Barbie held her breath and waited for him to come out. In less than a minute, the door opened again, and the figure came out carrying a carton. Barbie watched as he rested the box on one hip and opened the emergency exit with his free hand. Then he disappeared. Barbie decided to wait a minute or two to see if he'd come back.

Just as she was about to give up and go meet Christie, the thief returned and entered the room again. He came out carrying another box. On his next two trips, Barbie checked her watch and kept track of how long he stayed outside. Would she have enough time between trips to run down the hall and peek into the room before he got back? She watched the second hand on her watch go around completely four times. *Four minutes,* she thought. *I think I can make it.*

To her dismay, the thief came back right before she was about to run down the hall. But this time he pulled the room door closed behind him. Just as he was about to lock the door, his cell phone rang. Barbie strained her ears to hear what he was saying, but the hallway was too long and the soundproof walls muffled the sound. All she could catch were parts of sentences in a soft, muted voice. "Got 'em . . . four boxes . . . orders . . . fill . . . plenty more where these . . . It's in the bag. . . . Gotta hurry . . . the show . . ."

The phone conversation ended suddenly and the figure rushed out the exit door. Barbie's nose for news brought her out of the practice room and down the hall to the locked room. In his rush to get out, the mysterious man had left the key in the lock!

Feeling certain he'd discover his mistake and be back any minute, Barbie quickly opened the door and stepped inside. Just to be on the safe side,

46

she took a business card from her pocket, folded it into a small square, and stuffed it into the jamb to keep the door from locking. In the glow of the red light from the hallway, Barbie saw boxes stacked against the wall. On the side of each box the words SPIN PRODUCTIONS were stamped in big red letters. Barbie took a step forward, and her foot slipped on a piece of paper. She picked it up, and a quick glance showed her it was a packing slip describing the contents of the boxes. In the left-hand column on the sheet it said 500 CDS. In the center column it identified the title of the CDs — THE JAMMERS, THIS YEAR'S WINNER OF *THE BATTLE OF THE BANDS* — DISTRIBUTED BY SPIN PRODUCTIONS!

Barbie's eyes widened. *Didn't Corey say nobody knows who the winner is until the battle is over?* she thought.

Barbie pried open the flap on one of the boxes. Just as she feared, inside were well-packaged CDs, each labeled THE JAMMERS, THIS YEAR'S WINNER OF *THE BATTLE OF THE BANDS.*

Stuffing the packing slip in her pocket, Barbie grabbed the business card from the lock and got out fast. She closed the door behind her and ran on tiptoe back to the other end of the hallway. Just as she reached the steel door at her end, the emergency exit door opened at the other end. Barbie made it out just in time!

But now I've got some serious work to do, Barbie thought. *Someone's decided that the Jammers are going to win this contest. And I have a feeling that someone might be out to get 4 to Go!*

Chapter 9

• •

SURPRISES

"Thank goodness you're back!" Christie whispered as Barbie slipped back into her seat in the
auditorium. "I got my press pass back!"

The audience was applauding and Mike was
thanking Tuned Out for their fine performance.
"Where did you find it?" Barbie asked, completely
surprised.

Over the applause, Christie filled Barbie in. "The
kid with my pass ran up the aisle. He must have
dropped it on his way out. One of the ushers
brought it to me after Clyde told her where I was
sitting."

"What?" Barbie gasped. "Then I must have followed the wrong person. But I found something . . ."

Before she could finish her sentence, Mike

asked the audience for their close attention. "I have an important announcement," he said, holding up a sealed envelope. "Our judges have cast their votes and we have the finalists from today's *Battle of the Bands*."

The audience cheered in anticipation as Mike slowly opened the envelope. He read over the names first, and Barbie was certain he looked completely surprised by the results. "Ladies and gentlemen," he said, "I have to admit the results are not at all what I expected, but with so many great bands to choose from, it couldn't have been an easy decision to make. Are you ready to hear who will be coming back for tomorrow's battle?"

The audience shouted, "Yes!"

Mike laughed. "Okay," he said. "The finalists are — in third place, So Low; in second place, Tuned Out; and tied for the number one spot, the two groups that will fight to the finish on tomorrow's *Battle of the Bands*, the Jammers and 4 to Go! Unfortunately, equipment problems will keep 4 to Go out of the contest, so the battle will have to be between the Jammers and Tuned Out. May the best band win!"

"What?" Christie exclaimed, along with most of the audience. "How can that be?"

"I'm afraid someone is trying to rig the contest," Barbie replied, shaking her head. She quickly explained what she'd seen in the locked room. "Unless we can do something to stop it," she continued, "the Jammers are going to win *The Battle of the Bands*. Someone picked the winner before the battle even began! And if I'm right, whoever rigged the contest has plans to make a lot of money from the sale of the winning group's CD."

"Can't we stop it before it happens?" Christie asked. "We could tell Clyde or Mike or the police!"

"Not yet," Barbie said seriously. "First we need real proof. The packing slip will only be meaningful if I can find out who was carrying those boxes outside the building. Let's go back to the inn after the show. I want to put my notes in order and see what I've got so far."

"Okay," Christie said. "You go on ahead. I'm going to stop at the photo shop and leave my film to be developed. I want to make sure I've got the shots you need to go with your story. See you back at the room."

51

The girls split up and Barbie headed back to the inn alone.

As she was unlocking the door to her room, the phone rang. Barbie ran to answer it and was surprised to hear Jake Colton's voice. He was talking very fast and sounded upset.

"Thank goodness I reached you," he said urgently. "I hope you don't mind me calling you, but you're a reporter and I need your help. I've made a very disturbing discovery. Can you meet me at the performing arts center right away?" he asked.

"I'll be there in ten minutes," Barbie said, grabbing her jacket and her notebook. She left a quick note for Christie at the front desk, then started out, walking as quickly as she could.

Barbie reached the arts center in less than ten minutes. Jake Colton was waiting for her by the front entrance. "Thanks for coming so quickly," he said, holding the door for her. As he led the way to the stage of the auditorium, he explained his reason for calling her. "Someone messed with all the wires on the amplifiers and the cords on the guitars," he said. "Even the keyboard's wires were frayed in the middle. I think someone cut them on purpose!"

As soon as Barbie saw the wires that Jake held up, she knew Kira had been right. The damage was no accident.

"This is terrible!" Barbie exclaimed. "This must be brought to the attention of the production manager and the authorities."

"I tried talking to Clyde already," Jake said. "He seemed to think I was just being a poor sport about what he called 'the band's bad luck.' He said there was nothing he could do about it. I called you because you work for the newspaper. I thought if a reporter told the story, somebody might believe it."

"Jake," Barbie said seriously, "I believe you. And I think you are right. There is a story here, but it's bigger than just some cut wires. I have an idea. Can you and your band members show up for the battle tomorrow?"

"Sure!" Jake said. "But it's already been announced that we're out of the contest."

"You're going to play your song in the final battle tomorrow. And may the *real* best band win!" Barbie replied. "4 to Go isn't out of it yet! Meanwhile, you and the other guys need to borrow some equipment from one of the other bands. Can you take care of that by morning?"

Jake smiled. "You betcha!" he said. "If we get right on it, we should have no problem."

The two planned to meet in the morning, and Jake hurried off to tell the other guys in the band about the plan. Barbie was just about to leave when she had a thought — maybe there were more clues down at the dark end of the hallway. Maybe she could find something that identified the mysterious figure. He had to be connected to the Jammers somehow.

For the second time that day, Barbie entered the soundproof hallway and moved quickly toward the locked door. The hallway was as still as a tomb and felt airless to Barbie.

She slowed her pace as she neared the door and realized it was open. The key was in the lock. Even though the tones were absorbed by the soundproofing on the walls, Barbie heard two male voices. "It's not what it looks like," one voice said. "I swear, I don't know anything about it. But maybe you do!"

"Ha! Don't try to put this off on me," the other

voice growled. "Your career in this business is over. A scheme like this will ruin you!"

Barbie froze in her place. She recognized both voices. One voice belonged to Clyde, and the other voice belonged to Mike Parker! One of them was guilty and one of them was not. But which was which?

Suddenly, all the notes in her notebook ran through her mind — Clyde had nothing when he started out, Mike had said. Now he was in charge of everything — was he also in charge of 4 to Go's equipment? And was being in charge of "everything" not enough for him?

And Mike — he seemed so nice, but he'd actually had his own production company once. Did he still have it? And was he the man behind Spin Productions?

There was only one thing for Barbie to do. She reached out, quickly slammed the door shut, and turned the key in the lock! Then she ran for help. Behind her, she heard the two men shouting, "Let me out!"

Chapter 10

• • • • • • • • • • • • • • • • • • •

THE END OF THE BATTLE

Barbie emerged from behind the curtain and was surprised to find herself face-to-face with Christie and Jake Colton. "Barbie!" Christie and Jake exclaimed together.

"I've caught him!" Barbie gasped.

"Who?" Christie sputtered. "Caught who? I'm the one who caught someone. I just ran into Jake and he said he'd just left you. I brought the pictures with me to show both of you."

"Christie," Barbie repeated breathlessly, "I mean I've caught the guy who is fixing the contest so that the Jammers will win. We have to get the police!"

"Oh!" Christie exclaimed excitedly. "You mean you know who did it?"

"Mike Parker —" Barbie began.

56

"Mike Parker!" Christie gasped.

"Or Clyde Andrews," Barbie finished her sentence. "They're both locked in the room with the boxes. We have to get the police."

"Stop right where you are!" a voice boomed from the back of the theater.

The three looked up, and to their complete surprise, a police officer was walking down the aisle toward them. "You people aren't supposed to be in here now," the officer said sternly. "I followed you in here, young lady," he said directly to Christie. "I noticed your press pass and I have a report saying that same press pass was stolen! Hand it over and let's go down to the station!"

"But Officer," Barbie interrupted. "I'm Barbie Roberts from the *Willow Gazette*. And you're right, the press pass was stolen, but we recovered it earlier. This really is my photographer, Christie."

"Can you show me any proof that you're a photographer?" the officer asked Christie.

"Of course," Christie said with relief. She reached into her bag and pulled out the package of photos she'd just had developed. She handed them to the officer.

He looked through them carefully. "Not bad, except for this one," he said, handing them all back but one. He held a photo of a crowd scene. It was blurred and had no particular main subject. It was the photo Christie had taken by mistake when she'd been bumped in the crowd.

Barbie gasped, her eyes opening wide. "Officer!" she exclaimed, snatching the photo from his hand. "I think I may have just solved a real crime!"

Christie and Jake looked as stunned as the policeman. "What do you mean, Barbie?" Jake asked.

Barbie held out the photo. "Look!" Barbie said. "Do you see that black motorcycle on the road behind the crowd? Christie, we've seen that bike before. The license plate says SPIN PRO, and look who's driving the bike!"

"It's Clyde!" Christie breathed. "So he's the one who owns Spin Productions! And he's the one who delivered the CDs to the music stores and the radio stations!"

"And he's the one who tried to fix the contest so that the Jammers would win," Barbie finished.

"What's going on here?" the police officer asked.

"Good question!" Jake added.

"If you don't mind, Officer," Barbie replied, "follow me. I need you to arrest someone!"

Barbie explained everything to the officer as she led the way through the steel door and down the hallway to the locked room. They heard pounding on the door and the muffled cries of the two men locked inside. Barbie handed the key to the policeman, and she and Christie stepped back as he unlocked the door and swung it open.

"He did it!" both Mike and Clyde shouted, pointing at each other.

"I know exactly who did it," the policeman said. "Thanks to some clever detective work by a certain reporter and photographer from the *Willow Gazette.* The only mystery now is who will win *The Battle of the Bands* contest." He turned to Clyde. "You're under arrest."

Clyde shook his fist at Barbie and growled, "You ruined everything. The Jammers were gonna make it big and I was gonna make it bigger! I got those kids to sign a contract with me for nothing, and I was going to rake in the dough once they won!"

"Now it's going to be done fair and square," Mike promised as he, Barbie, Christie, and Jake followed the officer down to the police station to file a report.

Now that he'd been caught, Clyde admitted everything. He'd cut the wires and ruined the 4 to Go performance. He'd delivered scratched 4 to Go CDs to the radio stations. And he'd gotten the Jammers to record a full CD in advance so it would be ready to ship out as soon as the winner of the battle was announced.

"But Barbie, what about my stolen press pass?" asked Christie.

"At first I thought that was part of the mystery, too," said Barbie. "But now I think that boy just found it on the ground and used it to get into the concert."

"He did seem to be quite a music lover," Christie agreed.

Jake laughed. "I owe that kid a thank-you! If it wasn't for him, you never would've gone backstage and discovered those CDs, Barbie."

"Well, maybe you can give him your autograph,"

Barbie teased. "Now that we've caught the saboteur, you're sure to make it big!"

"And what about the Jammers? Did they put Clyde up to this?" asked Christie.

"I don't think so," said Barbie slowly. "I think Clyde really wanted them to be a success, but he just picked the wrong band. I mean, sure, the Jammers may not be the most pleasant guys, but that's not a crime."

"Maybe not, but their song should be!" said Christie, laughing.

As they all left the station, Mike stepped forward. "Congratulations, everyone," he said. "It looks as if you all came out winners in this battle. Barbie, you win for finding the best story behind *The Battle of the Bands.* Christie, you win for taking a photograph that's sure to help put a criminal behind bars. And Jake, even though the Jammers were not aware of any of the things Clyde was doing to make them win, they will be disqualified for agreeing to make a full CD for Clyde. The rules say the winner of the battle is not allowed to have released a full debut CD before the battle. So, you know what that means — you and the rest of the guys in 4 to Go will go up against Tuned Out tomorrow on the last day of *The Battle of the Bands*."

The next morning, Barbie and Christie took their front-row seats and waited for the concert to begin. Once again, a director spoke through a headset microphone to the crew in charge of filming. "Okay, music intro on three, and roll film! One . . . two . . . three!"

The audience applauded and Mike ran onto the stage. "Welcome back, music fans," he said, smiling into the camera. "Welcome to the final day of *The Battle of the Bands*! I'm sorry to say that due to legal issues, the Jammers have been disqualified. But I am glad to say that 4 to Go is now back in the competition. So, ladies and gentlemen, meet the final contenders in *The Battle of the Bands*, Jake Colton, Ace Frye, Kevin Taylor, and Dave Williams! Let's hear it for 4 to Go!"

The curtain swept up, and there was 4 to Go, singing their hearts out. *"You are my dream. You are my special one. Promise you'll stay forever and a day. I saw your face. And I knew right away.*

Our love would last forever and a day. Now that you're here and I am glad to say, I will love you forever and a day."

"I just know they're going to win," Barbie whispered to Christie.

Christie nodded. "How could they not?"

The applause began even before the band was finished singing. Jake Colton smiled at Barbie as he crooned the last notes of the song that would make 4 to Go the next music superstars.

"Thanks a lot!" Jake said over the applause. "Thanks, everyone! And a special thanks to Barbie Roberts for making this performance possible! Don't forget, Barbie and Christie, dinner's on us tonight!"

Barbie and Christie looked at each other and laughed. Barbie could feel herself blushing. She and Christie stood up with the rest of the audience and applauded until the band came back for an encore.

"I could listen to them play forever!" Christie shouted over the applause.

Barbie kept clapping as she laughed and replied, "Forever? I think you mean *forever and a day*!"

Reporter's Notebook

Can YOU solve the mystery of *Mystery Unplugged*? Read the notes in Barbie's reporter's notebook. Collect more notes of your own. Then, YOU solve it!

Story Assignment: *The Battle of the Bands* television show is being filmed at All State University. Attend the battle, meet the bands, report on the winner.

● ●

Background Info:
• Local bands are competing for the grand prize — a recording contract from Kingston Studios. The band that wins is guaranteed to make it big.
• The Jammers vs. 4 to Go — the Jammers are already getting plenty of radio airplay. 4 to Go's CDs are scratched and can't be played all the way through.

Mystery:
Who: Who is sabotaging 4 to Go? Who is the fan in the gray sweatshirt? Who is behind Spin Productions?

What: What does the press pass thief have to do with the locked room at the end of the hall?

How: How did the Jammers get so much publicity?

Where: Where is the clue that will solve the mystery?

Why: Why were Mike Parker and Clyde Andrews in the soundproof room?

Facts and Clues:

- Stranger on motorcycle with SPIN PRO license plate at music store
- Clyde worked his way up
- 4 to Go, talented guys who work hard
- The Jammers, six guys with little talent intent on winning and sure they will
- Christie's photos

Suspects:

- Fan in gray sweatshirt
- The Jammers — mean guys who are sure they'll win
- Mike Parker
- Clyde Andrews

Additional Notes:

Clue #1 _____
_____
_____

Clue #2 _____
_____
_____

Clue #3 _____
_____
_____

Clue #4 _____
_____
_____

Clue #5 _____
_____
_____

Clue #6 _____
_____
_____

Now YOU Solve It!

_____

_____

_____

_____

_____

_____

_____

_____

_____

_____

_____

_____

_____

_____

_____

_____

_____

_____

_____

_____

_____

_____

_____

CONGRATULATIONS from BARBIE! You are an Official Star Reporter and Mystery Solver! Sharpen your mystery-solving wits and get ready to help Barbie solve her next big case.